W9-CNW-532

Impatient Pamela

Calls 9-1-1

Dedicated to my children

M. Koski

Dedicated to Amaliea

D. Brown

Trellis Publishing, Inc.
P.O. Box 16141
Duluth, MN 55816

Impatient Pamela Calls 9-1-1

Publisher's Cataloging-in-Publication
(Provided by Quality Books, Inc.)

Koski, Mary (Mary B.)
Impatient Pamela Calls 9-1-1 / by Mary Koski ; illustrated by Dan Brown. -- 1 st ed.
p. cm.
SUMMARY: Young Pamela learns to use the telephone and to recognize an emergency, so when her friend is choking, she is able to dial 9-1-1 to summon emergency medical assistance.
Preassigned LCCN: 98-90206
ISBN 0-9663281-9-1

1. Telephone--Emergency reporting systems--Juvenile fiction. 2. Emergency medical technicians--Juvenile fiction. 3. Patience--Juvenile fiction. I. Brown, Dan (Daniel Seaton) II. Title. III. Title: Impatient Pamela calls nine one one.

PZ7.K85Im 1998 [E]
QBI98-361

Impatient Pamela Calls 9-1-1

text by Mary Koski

Illustrated By Dan Brown

Pamela was very impatient.

She always wanted to learn new things RIGHT NOW!

One day, she and Martin played in piles of leaves. They had a wonderful time flinging leaves high up in the air.

That night, Pamela's hair was full of little tree branches and leaves.

"Momma, will you teach me how to put my hair in a ponytail so it doesn't get so tangled?" Pamela asked.

"I suppose you are old enough to learn that. I'll show you tomorrow."

“May I do it now, Momma? Please?” Pamela asked.
“Tomorrow is soon enough Pamela. Off to sleep now.”
“Tomorrow, tomorrow. I always have to wait for tomorrow,” Pamela said sleepily as her cat, Meow-Man, curled up at her feet. She dreamt of leaves, and branches, and climbing trees, and tangle-free hair.

The next morning, Pamela's mother taught her how to comb her hair back, how to hold all of her hair in one clump with one hand, and how to put on the hair band. Pamela was thrilled -- she had a ponytail.

That night, her mother said, "I think it is time you learned your address."

"May I do it now, Momma?" Pamela begged, already knowing that she lived on Rainbow Drive.

"No, we'll start in the morning."

With Meow-Man at her feet, Pamela dreamt about addresses that rhymed with rainbow, like stain row, and plain black crow, and fainting arrow.

The next morning her mother said their address aloud, over and over again. By lunchtime, Pamela could remember every word.

Pamela went to play with Martin. They played in piles of leaves, they climbed trees in Martin's back yard, and they had snacks on Martin's back steps. Every now and then, Pamela would remember her address.

Pamela told Martin her address. Martin knew his own telephone number.

“Well, Pamela,” her mother asked her that evening, “can you remember your address?”

Pamela said her address loudly.

Her mother kissed Pamela’s cheek. “That’s my girl!” she said proudly.

Pamela wanted to learn how to use the telephone. "Martin knows his own telephone number! Pleeeaaasse may I?" she pleaded.

"Okay Pamela, I'll teach you tomorrow."

"Promise?" asked Pamela, hoping her mother wouldn't forget.

"Promise," said Pamela's mother.

That night, Pamela dreamt of addresses, and telephone numbers, and calling Martin to invite him over to play.

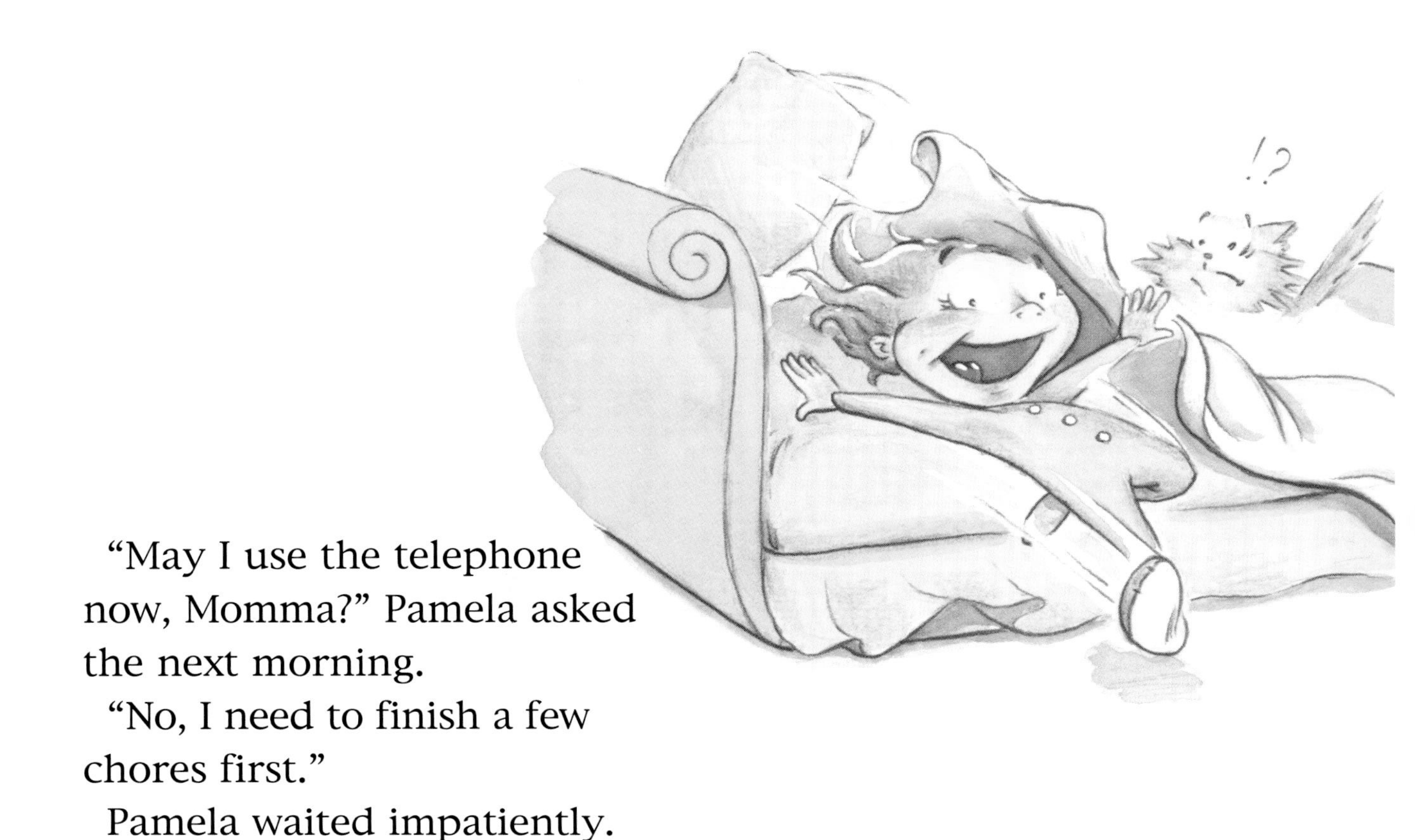

"May I use the telephone now, Momma?" Pamela asked the next morning.

"No, I need to finish a few chores first."

Pamela waited impatiently.

She sat and stared at the telephone, tapping her fingers on all the buttons, and pulling on the telephone cord.

She waited . . .

and waited.

She twirled her ponytail around with her fingers.

She counted to ten in her mind.

"Can you reach the number keys?" Pamela's mother finally asked.

"Yes I can," said Pamela.

"First, you pick up the receiver and listen for a dial tone. Then you press the numbers you want to call."

"How will I know Martin's number?" asked Pamela, a little worried.

"When you are older, you can read numbers from the telephone book. For now, here are some important numbers."

"May I call that one, Momma? 9-1-1?" Pamela asked.

"No, you may only press 9-1-1 if you need help. You may call Martin though."

So Pamela called Martin, and they had a good talk.

That night, with Meow-Man at her feet, Pamela dreamt of telephone books, and chalkboards, and numbers, and flashing buttons.

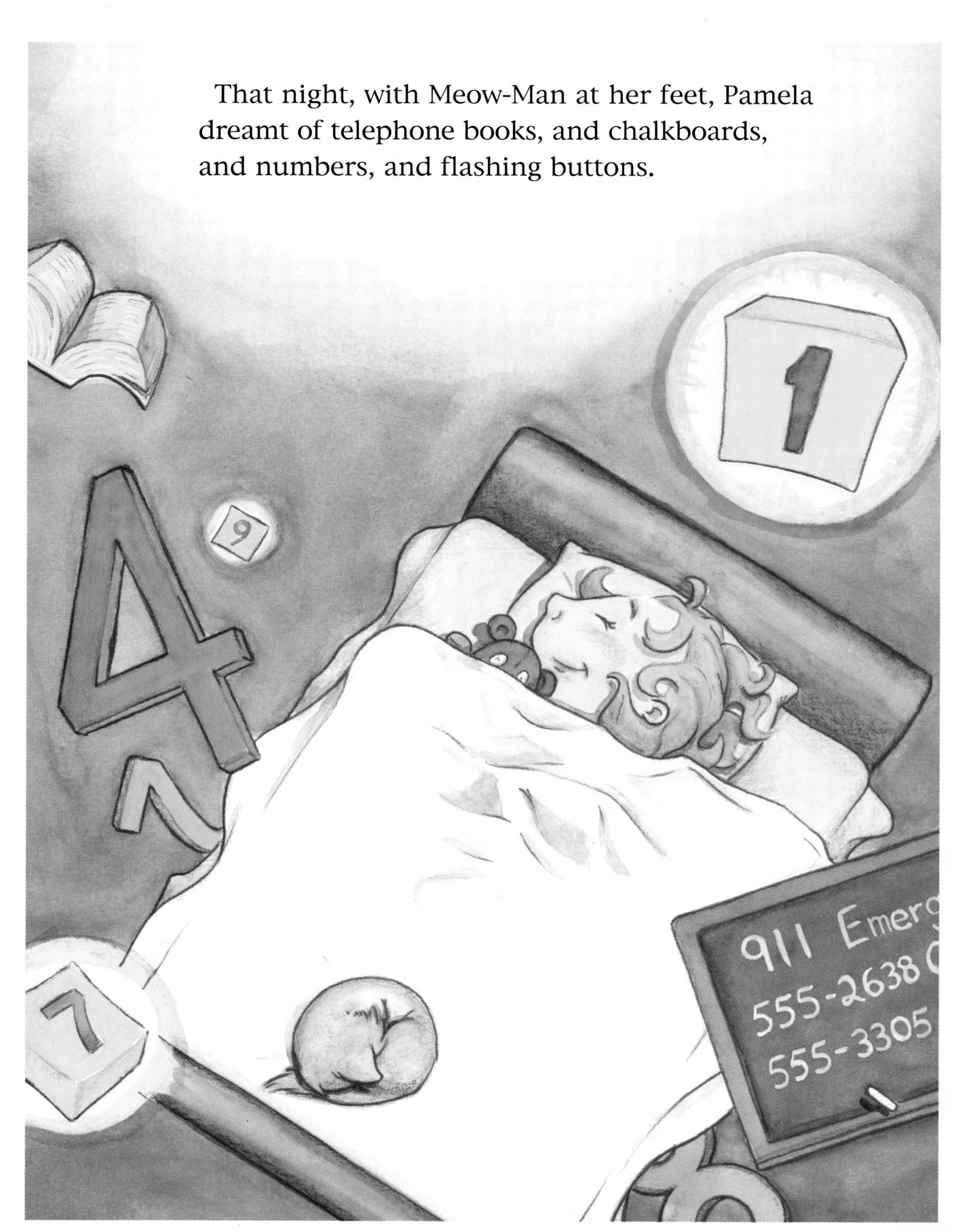

The next morning, Pamela saw a cat in a tree. She ran in the house.

"Momma, there's a cat in the tree next door. May I call 9-1-1 now, Momma?"

"No," said Pamela's mother, "the cat will jump down all by itself. It doesn't need help."

Pamela frowned. Then she saw her neighbor, Jessica, trying to push a broken bicycle.

"Momma, Momma," Pamela called. "Jessica's bicycle is broken. May I call 9-1-1? May I do it now, Momma?"

"No, you may only call 9-1-1 when a person needs help. Jessica's bicycle doesn't need 9-1-1."

Pamela was disappointed. She was impatient to call 9-1-1.

Martin came over and he and Pamela had sandwiches at the picnic table. Suddenly Martin choked on a bite of his sandwich, and he couldn't make any noise.

Pamela ran to her mother. “Momma, somethings wrong with Martin.”

Pamela’s mother rushed to Martin and patted his back, but he still could not breathe very well. She did the Heimlich squeeze, which helps people who are choking, but it wasn’t working on Martin.

“What can I do, Momma?” cried Pamela.

“Call 9-1-1,” her mother instructed, “and stay calm!”

Pamela hurried to the telephone. She pressed 9-1-1, very carefully. A woman's voice answered the phone.

"9-1-1, do you have an emergency?"

"I do," answered Pamela as bravely as she could. "My friend is choking, and my mother is trying to help him, but he can't breathe."

"Do you know the address?"

"Yes! 1405 Rainbow Drive."

"Help is on the way, but don't hang up the phone."

Soon a truck with flashing lights arrived, and the helpers got Martin to breathe again. They took Martin to the hospital to make sure he was okay.

When Martin came home, Pamela got to bring him some ice cream.

That night, when her father put Pamela to bed, he said "It's a good thing you learned how to dial 9-1-1."

"I'm glad I knew how Daddy."

"So am I, Pamela. You did a brave thing." He kissed her cheek and tucked her in.

Pamela dreamt of flashing lights, and ice cream, and dialing 9-1-1. Meow-man purred away at her feet.